THE TYRELL SHOW

SeaSoN TWO

WRITTEN BY MILES GROSE

ILLUSTRATIONS BY THE DIZZY DEVILS WITH ARTFUL DOODLERS

Scholastic Inc.

© 2023 Scholastic

All rights reserved. Published by Scholastic Inc., *Publishers since 1920.* SCHOLASTIC and associated logos are trademarks and/or registered trademarks of Scholastic Inc.

This book is a work of fiction. Names, characters, places, and incidents are either the product of the author's imagination or are used fictitiously, and any resemblance to actual persons, living or dead, business establishments, events, or locales is entirely coincidental.

ISBN 978-1-338-76723-0

1 2022
Printed in the U.S.A.   23
First printing 2023
Book design by Katie Fitch
Cover art by Shaz Enrico Lym
Interior artwork by The Dizzy Devils
with Artful Doodlers

To my incredible wife Lisa, my amazing stepdaughter Joelle and my adorable cat Tommy - you make me a better person every day... and one of you scratches me a lot.

—MG

EPISODE ONE:
WELCOME BACK

Hey, everyone! Welcome back! For those of you who know me, my name is still Tyrell and I'm the host of the highest-rated brain cast there is! And for those of you who don't know me, my name is Tyrell Edwards and I am, in my mother's words, the handsome and dynamic—her words not mine—host of *The Tyrell Show*!

The Tyrell Show is a kind of podcast that I do in my head. Oh, and do you remember before when I mentioned that it is "the highest-rated brain cast"? Yeah, well, if I'm being honest, it's actually the only one that I know of. That being said, maybe you know one? If you do, I think that's great!

On this brain cast, I introduce you to a lot of my favorite people . . . and some of my not-so-favorites. I'm looking at you, Shelly! People who know me know who I'm talking about, and so does Shelly. Anyway, I also share some of my experiences and even some of my thoughts and feelings about those experiences. Really though, I just have fun sharing, and I hope you have fun listening!

Oh, and I'm really excited about this new season! As I get older, I'm starting to see things differently. Like, I'm starting to understand why I should make my bed every day. I mean, my mom has always gotten on me about that! But the way I look at it is why make my bed when I'm just going to mess it up again at night?

Last week, I was at school and felt sick, like all nauseous and stuff! It was terrible! The only good thing about it was that I kept pretending that I was going to throw up on Shelly! I mean, if I was really gonna, that would've been nasty, but if I did, I mean by accident and whatnot, it would've been classic! Anyway, my mom came to school, picked me up, and took me to my room. Here's the thing: I hadn't made my bed that day, and I thought she was going to see that and get mad at me! But when I got into my room, it was a miracle . . . my bed was made! I was so sick and delirious I imagined that some magical mice made my bed, but the truth was, my mom did, and boy, was I glad she had done that!

It felt so good to get into my made bed! And even though I was really sick and delirious for the next few days . . . I mean, I imagined that the mice came back because one of them lost something while they were making the bed and now they were digging all around me to find it . . . Even though I had to go through all that, I was so happy to be in my nice bed with my clean new sheets and pillowcases. I even think the mice liked it.

*   *   *

Where was I? Oh yeah, I'm really excited about this new season because I decided to make a few upgrades to the show. As you may already know, I broadcast from my state-of-the-art brain studio, and it's really great! I mean, it's comfortable, and there are always snacks, imaginary but delicious. But as my dad always says, "Tyrell, success is good, but don't rest on your laurels."

Now, I've never quite been sure what that means. I looked up the word "laurels," and it had two definitions: One is like awards or success, and the other is a plant. I'm not sure why someone would rest on a plant, unless they were stranded on a desert island or something. And even then you would have to be careful what plant you lie on.

I remember one time me and my best friend, Boogie, cut

through a park on our way to school and he found a plant that he swore was mint. I mean, he was sooooo sure of it! He said his grandfather used to make tea with it, and he remembered the smell. He just sat there sniffing that plant forever, so finally I was like, "Come on, Boogie, we're gonna be late for school!" So he picked some of the plant, and we headed off to school! I'm just going to cut to the end of the story. Half our class, including us, had to miss a week of school because that plant wasn't mint. It was poison ivy!

I mean, sure, the story had a happy ending, who wouldn't like a week off from school, but I'm just saying . . . Wait, what was I saying? Oh yeah, I'm pretty sure when my dad says "resting on your laurels," he means your accomplishments, not a plant.

Uh-oh, I have some chores to do around the house! I hate chores—I mean, it's a Saturday, and after a long week of tests and arguing with friends and terrible school lunches and teachers giving way too much homework, you would think I could get a little break. Some cool video games, a slice or three of pizza, and a nice nap on the couch, but I guess that's too much to ask. You know, it's like the other day . . .

Dag, I was hoping to get to my chores before she called me! Okay, gotta go, but I'll be back to tell you about this new feature I added to my brain cast. Definitely come back—I promise I won't be long.

EPISODE TWO:
UPGRADES

Ugh, chores. Am I right? About the only thing I enjoy about chores is vacuuming and that's only because of how much Monty hates the vacuum! I mean, he really hates it! He barks at it like it stole his lunch money, which wouldn't be a good thing because Monty loves to eat! As a matter of fact, if Monty sees the vacuum when it's not plugged in, he tries to eat it.

Although I don't think he wants to eat it because he thinks it looks tasty! Um, BTW, in case you don't know and you didn't guess it, Monty is my dog. LOL, I just pictured you thinking that Monty was like my weird brother or sister!

First of all, I don't have a brother, and secondly, while my sister,

Al, is weird, she's not THAT weird! But imagine that . . . Which brings me to what I've been trying to tell you about! I want to introduce you to a new segment that I'm trying out on my show called "What If?!" Let me explain it to you. Have you ever been sitting somewhere and started daydreaming wild things like "What if it rained lemonade?" That would be great because if it started raining and you were thirsty, all you would have to do is run outside with a cup and catch some lemonade rain.

Only, don't look up because I think the lemonade would probably burn your eyes! Or, even better, "What if you owned your own ice-cream truck?" Okay, that would be amazing, right? I mean, if you could have ice cream anytime you want and if you ever need money, you could pull up to some kiddie playground and sell all the ice cream that you don't like to the little kids. Little kids will eat anything.

* * *

Anyway, I'm going to use my new segment to make "What If?" things come to life. For example, "What If Al Was Afraid of Vacuums?" And now please enjoy.

So that's "What If?" What do you think? Pretty cool, huh? Hey, I'm hungry, so I'm going to go and make some pizza. And yes, I know how to make pizza. I'm kind of a chef. You just take the frozen pizza out of the freezer and put it in the toaster oven at 425 degrees for ten minutes. I know some people like to put their frozen pizza in the microwave, but those people are amateurs. Anyway, I'll be right back with another episode.

EPISODE THREE:
MY COHOST

I'm back. I figured I have ten minutes to wait for my pizza, so I might as well do another episode. Plus, I have a lot to tell you. Now, I know I mentioned him earlier, but in case you don't know, I have a cohost. Well, actually a part-time cohost. Well, actually an unofficial part-time cohost. His name is Derek Lacey, but everyone just knows him as Boogie. Really quick, Boogie is my best friend! He's funny and generous and silly and really big for his age, but he wouldn't hurt a fly and not just because he's afraid of them. Actually, he's afraid of most things.

A few months ago, he moved away, and we were both really sad about it. For some reason, we even got mad at each other over it. But in the end, we realized we weren't mad at each other at all. We were just confused about our feelings. That ever happen to you? Where you get mad at something or just feel angry or sad and don't know why?

Well, that's what happened to us, but then we talked to our parents about our feelings and then we eventually spoke to each other and then we felt better. We realized that we didn't have to say goodbye forever—we would just have to figure out how to keep our friendship going! One way is we talk all the time. And we have an app on our phones where we can see each other. As a matter of fact, he is about to call me in a bit . . . And I have a big surprise for him! I mean, it's like really big! Can you keep a secret? Seriously, can you? Some people say they can, but they really can't!

Al can't! I know that now. When I was little, she used to be able to trick me and tell me that she wouldn't tell Mom and Dad about something that I did. Like maybe I broke a lamp or something. I'm not saying I broke a lamp, but let's just say that maybe I did. Al would be like, "Don't worry, dummy. I won't tell." But then later on that day my parents would confront me about the lamp, and I would be thinking to myself, *How could they possibly know that I did it?* . . . *Al!* Huh? I smell something burning? OH NO, MY PIZZA! Tyrell out!

EPISODE FOUR:
IT WAS A GREAT PARTY, PART 1

Yup, I burned it! My mom always says if I put something in the toaster oven that I should stay there and watch it . . . but I don't always listen to her. Oh, and of course Al was there to make fun of me and my burnt pizza!

Unfortunately, I found out she's not afraid of vacuums. Anyway, as I mentioned to you before, I have something I need to tell you! I'm about to call Boogie with a big surprise. And I feel comfortable that you won't ruin the surprise and call him because I doubt you have Boogie's number. His mom doesn't let him give his number out! Okay, last week was my parents' twentieth anniversary. For you little kids, that means that they've been married, eww, for twenty years. The party was a lot of fun! There was food, and music, and cake . . . oh yeah, the cake. LOL! I'm going to tell you about the cake in a minute! But first, the party wasn't all good . . .

Al begged our parents for forever so that when she turned sixteen a month ago she could start dating. First of all, I have no idea why anyone would want to date. But more than that, why would anyone want to date Al?! Have you seen her in the morning? And have you smelled her breath?! Anyway, so Al, thinking she's all grown now, brought her new booooyfriend to the party, and what a weirdo! His name is William, but I call him "Weird Willie," not to his face or anything. I mean, he is in the tenth grade, and I don't need that kind of heat, but I definitely call him that when I'm talking to Al. And she has definitely told on me to my parents about it. And they have definitely spoken to me about it! But I definitely believe they think he's weird too.

Willie is always asking me questions about Al, like "What does she like to eat?" "What's her favorite color?" "What's her favorite flower?" Hey, Willie, I have a question for you—"Why would I know or care about any of that?!" Oh, and he's always calling me "big guy," even though he's, like, a foot taller than me.

*　*　*

The other bad thing about the party is that my parents are friends with the Douglasses, and the Douglasses happen to be the parents of my archenemy Smelly Shelly Douglass! Her name is actually just Shelly Douglass. I gave her the "Smelly" part . . . and trust me, she is. Don't get me wrong, I don't make up mean nicknames for everyone, really just Weird Willie, Smelly Shelly, oh yeah, and Al. I mean, Al's real name is Alexandra, and she hates that I call her Al. But Al's not really a nickname, it's more of an abbreviation, so Weird Willie and Smelly Shelly are the only two. That's not so bad. Is it?

But worse than all that, back to Smelly. If you know me, you know that we have been rivals since first grade! She has spent her life trying to embarrass me! She has even sent girls "love notes" from me! Can you believe that? "If you like me, check 'yes.'" And she has told on me to the teacher so often that when she raises her hand in class, the teacher just says, "Yes, Shelly, what has Tyrell done now?"

Anyway, all us kids were in the kid section of the party, and Willie and Al were being all lovey-dovey when all of a sudden Weird Willie says out loud for everyone to hear, "Hey, Tyrell! You and Shelly would make a cute couple." I know, right?! As if! And then before I could say "EW," Shelly spit out the punch she was drinking and let out a really long and dramatic "EWWWW!!" And of course everyone laughed. Yeah, thanks a lot, Weird Willie and Smelly Shelly!

EPISODE FIVE:
IT WAS A GREAT PARTY, PART 2

Okay, I just told you two bad things about the party. Now I want to tell you two amazing things. Wow, which one should I tell you first? They're both pretty good! I know—you choose! One has to do with Boogie, and the other has to do with Monty. Which one? I feel like I can hear you yelling, "Monty!" I mean, he is an adorable dog, and who doesn't like funny dog videos and memes? And it is a really good story!

So when my dad was giving his speech about how much he loves my mom and telling stories about how they met and stuff that happened when I was younger, you know boring stuff... Monty, who wasn't paying attention to my dad, started eyeing this big cake someone made for their anniversary. And here's the thing, while everyone but Monty was paying attention to my dad, no one was paying attention to Monty. Big mistake!

I kind of saw it all happen in slow motion. Monty started running toward the cake at full speed! I saw him, but I wasn't close enough to stop him. By this time, everybody could see what was happening, but no one could get to him. Then, all of a sudden, he made a leap for the cake! And at first, it looked like he began his jump too soon, like he wasn't going to be able to make it to the cake. I mean, if I'm being honest, Monty could stand to lose a few pounds. Plus, his legs are pretty short! I'm just saying, he is not built for long jumps!

But halfway through his jump, at the point where he probably should have started to fall to the ground, it looked like he got some sort of doggy rocket boost, and he just kept going! And before you know it, to everyone's surprise, he landed right in the middle of the cake! I think it even surprised Monty because, instead of enjoying his jump, he just started scrambling, which was bad because his little legs were flailing around as pineapple upside-down cake flew everywhere! I know it was pineapple upside-down cake because some of it flew in my mouth. It was really good, but then again, I love pineapple upside-down cake.

Anyway, Monty took one bite, then jumped down and ran! It was hilarious, although I don't think my mom and dad thought it was very funny. But you should've seen it! Monty, covered in cake, was being chased by all these adults. They were just trying to catch him to wash him off, but Monty hates baths, so he wasn't having it. Finally, Al called him, so he was going to go to her, but Weird Willie, I guess trying to be her hero, stepped in front of her, and Monty, who had already jumped to be in Al's arms, landed in Willie's arms. As I said, Monty is not the skinniest dog, so that knocked Willie to the ground. Now Monty is on top of Willie, and Willie says, "There you go, big guy. I got you." If there's one thing I know about Monty, it's that if he runs around too much after he eats . . . he throws up . . . which he did . . . all over Willie. Take that, big guy! Told you it was a good story!

* * *

Okay, now the Boogie one. On the morning of my parents' anniversary, I wanted to do something special for them, so I made them breakfast in bed . . . Wait, that doesn't even sound right. I made breakfast in the kitchen and then brought it to them in bed. Ha! Imagine if I actually made breakfast in bed!

Yeah, that wouldn't be good. Anyway, I made some waffles in the toaster and some microwave sausages. Oh, and I poured them some almond milk and orange juice. And if I'm being honest, Al helped me. I mean, she can be nice sometimes and since it was my parents' anniversary, I guess she figured today would be a good day for one of those times. So then I took the breakfast up to my parents' room and surprised them with breakfast in bed, just like I do every year. I also gave them a card that I made myself, AND I put some money in it for them.

Yup, when I was a little kid, I used to get cards with money in them from adults, and I think now that I'm getting a little older I need to act more like an adult and give my parents some cash. Plus, they do so much for me. I mean, where would I be without them? Am I right? Well, after they thanked me for the ten dollars (I gave them two five-dollar bills so that it would be easy to split) and after they read their card but just before they ate their breakfast, they told me that they had a surprise for me.

Listen to this! They said they had spoken to Boogie's mom, and all of them had decided that it was time for me to finally go and see them! Yup! I'm going to see my best friend in the world! And I get to spend a whole week with him! And guess what else?! No guess? Time's up! I get to fly in an airplane! I love airplanes!

They fly so high and go so fast! And I've never flown on a plane, at least that I can remember. According to my parents, I flew somewhere when I was a baby. They said I cried the entire flight! I don't remember that. I probably didn't even know that I was on a plane. I bet if they told me that I was on a plane, I would've stopped crying. And I can promise you I won't be crying this time!

See, my parents are the best! I probably should have given them twenty dollars. Oh, snap! It's almost time for Boogie to call me! He doesn't know that I'm coming to visit him. Me and Monty are going to surprise him on the call. That reminds me, I have to go and get Monty! Boogie is supposed to call me in exactly ten minutes, so if you want to be a part of that very special moment, don't go anywhere. I'll be right back!

EPISODE SIX:
TEN A.M.!!

I'm back! I almost couldn't find Monty, but then I looked in my room and saw his butt sticking out from under my bed. He was trying to get one of my dirty socks that was under there, and he got stuck. It was really very funny to see. I took a picture of it on my phone. Look:

Hilarious, right?! Hey, don't mention to my mom how messy my room is . . . or the fact that I had a dirty sock under my bed . . . or the fact that Monty got stuck trying to get at it. She says the fact that I leave dirty socks around and the fact that Monty wants to play with them is disgusting. If you tell her anything, please mention how nicely I made my bed.

*   *   *

Okay, it's 9:58 and Boogie is supposed to call me exactly at 10:00 a.m. I made him promise to be exactly on time. See, I'm going to have Monty on my lap, and the two of us are going to make this face that really scares him. This is going to be great! Hey, I just thought about this—you just saw me imagining that I scared Al and now me and Monty are about to scare Boogie. I don't want you to think all I do is go around scaring people. I mean, I do lots of other things, even helpful things. Like, one time, my mom was sick and I made her some tea. And she really liked it. She said it would have been a lot better if I had remembered to put a tea bag in the water, but she still said, "This is the best-tasting water I've ever had!"

Anyway, overall I would say I'm pretty nice, but I have to admit, scaring people is hilarious! Uh-oh, it's 9:59. Excuse me a second. MONTY! Come on, it's time!

What was that all about? I mean, you heard all that, right? Was it me? Did I say something? I thought he would be so excited, but instead it seemed like he was . . . If I'm being honest, I don't know what he seemed like, but he definitely didn't sound like himself. Okay, like, he laughed at the funny thing that Monty and I planned for him and, yes, if anyone asks you, Monty and I definitely planned that moment when I fell. But it seemed like after that everything changed. I wonder if he's jealous about me getting to fly on a plane. We both love planes. Or maybe he just doesn't feel well? Maybe? Wait a minute. I feel like the whole conversation really changed when I mentioned his friends, especially Carl. I don't know a lot about him. I kind of remember when Boogie first got to his new place he talked about Carl a lot. But then, one day, he said something happened that he didn't feel like talking about. Hmm, now that I think about it, he never brought Carl up again. I wonder what it was? Well, anyway I can't wait to see Boogie! And to all my listeners out there, I promise to get to the bottom of this whole Carl thing! Okay, I had better go. I've been doing brain casts all day. See you soon!

EPISODE SEVEN:

FLYING SOLO WHILE FEELING SO LOW

Welcome back! Okay, a lot has happened since the last episode. If you remember, Boogie was acting really weird when I called him. At first, I was like, *That's just Boogie being Boogie,* but then I was like, *Boogie's weirdness is usually funny but that weirdness was just . . . well, weird.* So I decided to talk to my parents about it. In case you don't know, my parents and I are really close and I always feel like I can talk to them about anything. I mean, they've known me since I was a baby, so I would say they know me pretty well!

Anyway, I went looking for them and I saw my mom—actually, she saw me! She has this mom power where she always kind of knows when I need her, even sometimes before I do, which is pretty great and scary all at once. Oh, and she also knows when I'm lying, and there have even been times when she has stopped me right before I lied . . . now that's just plain scary!

So my mom came up to me and was like, "What's wrong, baby?" And, yes, she calls me "baby," and, yes, I allow it, and, yes, when I'm feeling down, I actually like it. That being said, if you write into the show, do NOT call me "baby"! Trust me, I will not respond. Okay, back to my story. I told my mom all about the call. I told her how Boogie was all laughing and stuff in the beginning but after I told him my big surprise about me coming to visit him, he got all quiet and weird. And she said that in life we never know what someone else is going through and that we always need to practice compassion. And then, when she could tell that I didn't really know what she meant, she explained it to me a little more.

To make things easier for me, she usually gives me an example that I can understand. I call them "Mini Explainin' Stories." I don't remember exactly what she said, but it definitely helped me understand. Want me to show you what I mean? I hope you said yes, because I've got a bunch of "What-If Brain Photos" to help you understand what I'm talking about.

YOU AND YOUR FRIEND GO TO AN ICE-CREAM PARLOR, AND YOU'RE ALL EXCITED BUT FOR SOME REASON HE'S NOT. HERE'S A PHOTO:

OKAY, SO NOW HERE'S A PHOTO OF YOU WITH AN INCREDIBLE ICE-CREAM CONE WITH TEN SCOOPS! AND IN THE PHOTO, YOU'RE LOOKING OVER AT YOUR FRIEND AND ASKING HIM IF HE'S GETTING ANYTHING, AND HE'S JUST KIND OF LOOKING AT YOU, SAYING NOTHING.

NOW, IN THIS ONE, YOU'RE THERE STARING AT YOUR ICE CREAM THINKING THIS IS JUST ABOUT THE BEST DAY OF YOUR LIFE AND THE ONLY THING RUINING IT IS YOUR FRIEND'S GRUMPY ATTITUDE. SO YOU'RE LOOKING AT HIM LIKE, *"IF YOU WEREN'T GOING TO GET ANY ICE CREAM, THEN WHY DID YOU COME WITH ME TO AN ICE-CREAM PARLOR?!"*

AND JUST AS YOU'RE ALL SET TO IGNORE HIS ANSWER AND JUST BE MAD AT HIM, HE TELLS YOU HOW HE WENT TO THE DENTIST THAT DAY BECAUSE HE HAD A TOOTHACHE AND HE WOUND UP GETTING A FILLING! I KNOW, RIGHT?! THAT'S BAD! SO THEN HERE'S A PICTURE OF YOU AT THE DENTIST GETTING A FILLING!! IF I'M BEING HONEST, I AM NOT A HUGE FAN OF THE DENTIST!

AND THEN YOUR FRIEND SAYS THAT THE ONLY REASON HE CAME WITH YOU IS BECAUSE HE WANTED TO SPEND TIME WITH YOU. OKAY, SO NOW NOT ONLY ARE YOU NOT MAD AT HIM ANYMORE, BUT YOU ALSO FEEL BAD FOR HIM. NOT TO MENTION THE FACT THAT YOU DON'T WANT THAT ICE-CREAM CONE ANYMORE BECAUSE, AS MY MOM SAYS, "SWEETS CAN CAUSE CAVITIES," AND THE LAST THING YOU WANT IS A CAVITY! SO IN THIS LAST PICTURE —ACTUALLY THIS ONE IS A BRAIN SELFIE— WE SEE THE SADDEST THING OF ALL.

And that's what showing compassion can look like. I don't think my mom was trying to tell me that Boogie had a toothache, but I do think she was trying to tell me to be mindful of the fact that I have no idea what he's going through. It's kind of like how last school semester Boogie and I had a misunderstanding where we wound up being mad at each other but then realized we weren't really mad at each other at all. What I learned from that experience was the best way to avoid a misunderstanding is to let others know what you're feeling and take the time to find out what they're feeling.

Now, just as I was really feeling good about myself for understanding my mom's story, my dad came in looking like he had some big news for me. I could tell it was going to be big because he called me High Speed. That's an old nickname he gave me when I was little because he said I could figure things out quickly. He hadn't called me that in a while, so I knew he had something for me that I would have to figure out! Um, yeah, I was definitely right!

And just like that, they let me know that I would be flying by myself, solo, on an airplane to visit Boogie. Am I a little scared? Yes. Am I very excited? An even bigger yes! First of all, I love airplanes! I mean, what's not to like? They go fast and travel way up into the sky and can take you anywhere.

Not like to outer space or to the bottom of the ocean but just about anywhere else. By the way, did you know that it's so dark at the bottom of the ocean that some fish have lights growing out of them? Do you know how useful that would be if you wanted to sneak to the kitchen in the middle of the night to get some snacks without anyone knowing?

Yeah, that would be pretty cool! Oh, and secondly, I get to see my best friend in the world—Boogie! Well, this day has been a lot and I'm feeling a little sleepy now, so I think I'll sign off. I'm not sure when I'm going to do my next episode, so stay tuned and I'll see you soon.

EPISODE EIGHT:
KICKING AND SCREAMING

Hello, everyone, and welcome to a new episode of *The Tyrell Show.* I know that sounded a little official, but I felt like I needed to do something special considering the fact that today I'm not doing my show from Brooklyn, New York. Nope, today I'm in Charleston, South Carolina, which is a long way from New York City.

Actually, it's 753 miles away, which feels kind of strange to me! I mean, I've never been that far away from my parents before. If I'm being honest, it's kind of making me sad to think about it, but on the plus side, I am 753 miles away from Al, so that's good.

As you know, I flew on an airplane—as a matter of fact, I'm still on it! Wild, right?! Sorry I didn't do my show earlier, but things got a little emotional this morning when my mom and dad dropped me off. I mean, there were so many tears, I swear I thought my dad was never going to stop crying! Oh, but don't tell him I told you that! Oh, and don't tell my mom I said "I swear." She hates that. Anyway, I was thinking about it when I boarded the plane, but I was so busy meeting Joy and Seth. They're the flight attendants who looked out for me during the flight, and they were really nice and looked really cool in their uniforms! Wanna see them? Here—look.

HERE'S ONE OF ME JUST AS I GOT ON THE PLANE. THAT'S JOY! SHE WAS REALLY NICE!

THEN! SHE TOOK ME TO THE COCKPIT... THAT'S WHERE THE PILOT AND COPILOT SIT AS THEY FLY THE PLANE! AND LOOK WHO I MET! THE PILOT! HER NAME WAS CAPTAIN CHERYL ANDERSON, AND SHE WAS DOUBLE, SUPER, STUPID NICE! SHE TOLD ME BECAUSE OF REGULATIONS THAT SHE COULDN'T ALLOW ME IN THE COCKPIT, BUT SHE OPENED THE DOOR AND LET ME LOOK IN. THERE WERE SO MANY BUTTONS AND DIALS —I'M TELLING YOU IT WAS WILD! SEE FOR YOURSELF!

THEN JOY INTRODUCED ME TO SETH. HE WAS REALLY TALL AND VERY FRIENDLY. SETH WAS THE ONE WHO TOOK ME TO MY SEAT! AND GUESS WHAT? I GOT TO SIT RIGHT BY THE WINDOW!

THEN A MAN AND A WOMAN SAT NEXT TO ME. I THINK THEY WERE, LIKE, BOYFRIEND AND GIRLFRIEND. I DON'T KNOW. THEY WERE NICE AND ALL AND ASKED ME QUESTIONS AND STUFF, BUT THE REST OF THE TIME THEY WERE ALL LIKE LEANING THEIR HEADS ON EACH OTHER AND HOLDING HANDS AND WHATNOT. I WAS GOING TO COMPLAIN ABOUT THEM TO SETH, BUT I DECIDED I DIDN'T WANT TO GET THEM IN TROUBLE OR ANYTHING.

ANYWAY, AFTER A WHILE, THE CREW MADE SOME ANNOUNCEMENTS, THEN TOLD US WHAT TO DO IN CASE THERE WAS AN EMERGENCY, AND THEN, RIGHT AFTER THAT, THE PLANE TOOK OFF...WHICH...WAS... *AMAZING!!* I SHOULD'VE DONE MY BRAIN CAST THEN, BUT IF I'M BEING HONEST, I WAS SO EXCITED THAT I DIDN'T EVEN THINK ABOUT IT! OH, AND THEN THEY BROUGHT ME SOMETHING TO DRINK, AND THEY HAD, LIKE, ANYTHING I WANTED! THEN THEY GAVE ME SOME SNACKS! I PROBABLY HAD, LIKE, THREE BAGS OF CHIPS AND FOUR GLASSES OF JUICE, I'M TELLING YOU EVERYTHING WAS GREAT...UNTIL...SOMEONE BEHIND ME KICKED MY CHAIR! THE FIRST ONE CAME OUT OF NOWHERE!

YUP, MY SNACKS WENT FLYING EVERYWHERE! THE COUPLE NEXT TO ME STOPPED HOLDING HANDS LONG ENOUGH TO CALL SETH FOR ME. SETH CAME OVER AND HELPED ME CLEAN UP AND THEN SPOKE TO THE PEOPLE BEHIND ME. THEY APOLOGIZED AND SAID THAT THEIR KID MUST HAVE DONE IT BY ACCIDENT. KIDS?! THEY CAN BE A HANDFUL! I MEAN, AM I RIGHT? SO ANYWAY, SETH OFFERED ME MORE SNACKS, BUT I PICTURED MY MOTHER SAYING, "YOU'VE HAD ENOUGH, TYRELL." SO I SAID, "NO, THANK YOU." SO LATER, I WAS SITTING THERE STARING OUT THE WINDOW AT THE CLOUDS WHEN ALL OF A SUDDEN THAT LITTLE KID KICKED MY SEAT AGAIN, THEN AGAIN AND AGAIN, AND THEN LIKE THIRTY-TWO TIMES MORE!

I WAS LIKE, "HEY, STOP THAT!" BUT HE DIDN'T! I LOOKED OVER AT THE COUPLE NEXT TO ME TO SEE IF THEY WOULD HELP, BUT THE LADY HAD HER HEAD ON HER BOYFRIEND'S SHOULDER AND THEY WERE ASLEEP! UGH! THEN I LOOKED BACK BETWEEN THE SEATS, AND I SAW THE FACE OF THE BAD LITTLE BOY WHO WAS KICKING MY CHAIR! HE HAD ONE OF THOSE FACES THAT MADE HIM LOOK TO HIS PARENTS LIKE HE'S A LITTLE ANGEL, BUT SOMEONE LIKE ME WHO UNDERSTANDS THESE THINGS KNEW BETTER. WHEN HE SAW ME, HE STOPPED KICKING FOR A MINUTE. I LOOKED OVER AT HIS PARENTS FOR HELP, BUT THEY WERE SLEEPING JUST LIKE THE COUPLE NEXT TO ME. UGH, COUPLES! ANYWAY, I LOOKED BACK AT HIM, AND WE LOCKED EYES. THEN HE HELD UP HIS LEG LIKE HE WAS GETTING READY TO KICK MY SEAT AGAIN. I GOT REALLY SERIOUS AND SAID, "DON'T YOU DARE!" AND DO YOU KNOW WHAT HE DID? HE SMILED AT ME!

AND THEN HE KICKED MY SEAT AS HARD AS HE COULD! SO HARD THAT HE ACTUALLY HURT HIS FOOT, STARTED CRYING, AND WOKE EVERYONE UP. WHEN HIS PARENTS WOKE UP, THEY KIND OF FIGURED OUT WHAT HE DID, SO THEY APOLOGIZED TO ME. OH, AND THE LITTLE KID GOT IN TROUBLE, SO AT LEAST THERE WAS A HAPPY ENDING! OTHER THAN THAT, THE REST OF MY FLIGHT WAS GREAT. ANYWAY, LIKE I SAID, I'M STILL ON THE PLANE. I HAVE TO WAIT UNTIL EVERYONE GETS OFF, AND THEN JOY IS GOING TO COME AND GET ME AND HELP ME GET OFF AND FIND BOOGIE AND HIS MOM. SO I GUESS I'LL END THIS EPISODE NOW, BUT DON'T GO ANYWHERE— THE BIG BOOGIE REUNION EPISODE IS NEXT, AND TRUST ME, YOU WON'T WANT TO MISS IT. HEY, BEFORE I GO, I JUST REALIZED I FORGOT TO SHOW YOU A PICTURE OF SETH...OH, AND... HOW COULD I FORGET THIS?! CAPTAIN ANDERSON GAVE ME A PIN WITH WINGS LIKE THE PILOTS WEAR ON THEIR UNIFORMS. SHE SAID SHE WAS GIVING IT TO ME FOR BEING SO BRAVE AND FLYING BY MYSELF! HERE'S A PICTURE OF ME, MY PIN, AND ALL OF TEAM "HELP TYRELL FLY." OH, AND I DECIDED TO MAKE THIS PHOTO A LITTLE SPECIAL! SEE YOU SOON!

EPISODE NINE:
THE GREAT BOOGIE REUNION

Hey, everyone! Oh my goodness, so much has happened since my last show! Like what, you ask? One word—BOOGIE! I was so happy to see him! And I think he was happy to see me! Joy was walking me through the airport and asking me stuff like did I enjoy my flight and what are some of the things I was looking forward to doing in Charleston when all of a sudden I heard "TYRELL!" And just as I turned to see where it was coming from, Boogie grabbed me, picked me up, and swung me around!

If I'm being honest, it was a little embarrassing . . . but if I'm being even honest-er . . . I kind of loved it! After he finally put me down, I saw his mom, Iris, and his little brother, Ricky, standing there. His mom said, "Hi, Tyrell," and then gave me a hug. Ricky ignored me, of course, but that was what he normally does and it didn't bother me at all because I was even happy, kind of, to see him. After that, I introduced them to Joy and then Joy hugged me goodbye. Joy and Seth were so nice! I hope they're on my flight when I go home. Hey, Seth and Joy, if you're listening, much love!

*   *   *

After that, Boogie told me to jump on his back because he wanted to give me a piggyback ride all the way to their car. Of course I hopped on, and it was fun for a bit, but we did not make it all the way to their car. As a matter of fact, we didn't make it very far at all. I mean, I'm definitely a lot heavier than I look, and I think Boogie is definitely out of "piggyback practice."

I didn't mind walking though. As a matter of fact, I really don't even remember walking through the airport at all! All I remember is that Boogie and I talked and laughed, and all I kept thinking was that Boogie doesn't look sad at all. Maybe he was just having a bad day when we spoke last. When I looked at him, all I saw was my big happy friend! And then, before we knew it, we were in the parking lot at their car . . . Only, it wasn't a car, it was a truck, and it wasn't theirs, it was Boogie's uncle Cutter's.

I had never met Uncle Cutter before, but Boogie has always

told me a lot of great stories about him. Uncle Cutter is Boogie's mom's brother, and he was the one that suggested that Boogie's family come back to South Carolina to live. Boogie's family is from South Carolina, only not Charleston where the plane landed. They're from another city called Columbia. Boogie's uncle Cutter has a farm there with cows and horses! Can you believe that?! Oh, and in case you're wondering, "Cutter" is not his real name—it's his nickname.

Boogie said he got that name because he's always cutting people off when they're talking. I know if I did that all the time I would just get in trouble! You've met my mom—you know she doesn't play that. Now like I said, since I knew that Uncle Cutter always cuts people off, I decided that when I spoke to him, I would talk really fast. That way he wouldn't have a chance to cut me off. So when I saw him, I went up to him, and just like my dad always told me to do, I reached out my hand to shake his! Right away, he grabbed my hand with his HUGE hand . . . I mean, it was gigantic! It was like a bear's paw! And then, right before I could say, "Hello, Uncle Cutter, my name is Tyrell," he said, "Hello there, Tyrell! It is a right pleasure to meet you!" Yup, he did it—he cut me off! Then he lifted up my heavy suitcase like it was nothing and put it in the back of his truck and said,

"WOOO! Come on, now, party people, let's get goin'!" My first impressions of Uncle Cutter are that he is part man, part bear, and part a lot of fun!

*   *   *

Anyway, like I said, they don't live in Charleston—they live in Columbia, which is like a two-hour ride away. So we all got in Uncle Cutter's big truck and started our drive from the airport in the city of Charleston to Boogie's house outside Columbia, which is, like Boogie says, "waaaay out in the country!" Now, while Boogie had told me that many times, I don't think I really believed him. I mean, when he lived in Brooklyn, he would say that going to Prospect Park was visiting the country.

But as we drove, I started to understand what he meant! First, there were, like, no more big buildings, just a lot of open space and stuff growing. I mean, I don't know what was growing because I'm not a farmer, but I bet there was corn and tomatoes and stuff. And then, all of a sudden, I started seeing cows and horses everywhere. Pretty amazing!!

*   *   *

Then we got to Boogie's house! OMG, Boogie's house is sooo big! Compared to where we live in Brooklyn, Boogie's new house is like a mansion! I think it's the house that Boogie's mom grew up

56

in. Anyway, I know I was really sad when Boogie's mom moved them away, but once I saw that house, I completely understood. Actually, don't tell anyone, but I was a little jealous! But I mean, you have to see Boogie's house! It has a big yard and a stream running behind it. The only type of stream I'm used to is the one that happens when someone opens a fire hydrant and sprays the water for us to run through during the summer.

Boogie used to visit this house during the holidays when his family would go to see his grandparents. In art class, he would always draw pictures of it, but if I'm being honest, Boogie's art skills aren't that great, so I could never understand what was so special about the house. I'm not trying to be mean—Boogie has many amazing skills, but art isn't one of them. Don't believe me? Check out one of Boogie's drawings of the house and one of the brain photos I took, and tell me what you think.

Okay, I think I made my point! Like I said, Boogie's new home is amazing! And he was about to take me around and show me everything when his mom told Boogie that he needed to let me get settled first. Adults always say things like "Go and get settled," and I don't actually know what that means. I guess it's a nice way to tell you to calm down. Oh, and "washing up" is usually a part of getting settled.

Hey, do you think when adults say that, it's a nice way for them to say "You smell"? It could be, because if I'm being honest, after my flight and that long car ride, I did kind of smell like three-day-old pizza.

*   *   *

After we both washed up, we went to Boogie's room to "settle down." After lying there for a little while, I think it kind of hit us again . . . We are together!! So we immediately started doing what we normally do! We started wrestling! Boogie immediately tried to squash me, but I rolled out quickly, got to the top of his bed, and went all airborne on him, and before I could land a perfect splashdown . . . his mother walked in.

I wanted to answer her by saying, "None of it," but I figured that might not go over very well. Now, even though she seemed pretty angry, she actually wasn't. She said, "I know you two are excited to see each other, but try to find appropriate ways to express it." Boogie's mom is the best!

*　*　*

After she left, we started thinking about things to do, and then it hit me . . . we need to go live with a special episode! I don't know how many of you know this, but for a long time, Boogie was always asking me if he could be my cohost on my brain cast and I would always say no. But after everything that happened between us last semester, I realized how important Boogie is to me and how extremely important it is to Boogie to be my cohost, and I finally decided to give him the job. And that's what's happening now.

Boogie's in the bathroom changing clothes because he said he wants to look great for his first show as cohost. I tried to stop him and tell him he looked fine, but . . . well, you know Boogie. And if you don't, you will soon! Okay, so I'm going to end this episode, and as soon as Boogie gets here, we'll go live! Stay tuned!

EPISODE TEN:
ALL THINGS BOOGIE

OH, YOU DID? THAT'S GREAT! SODA CITY IS A PRETTY COOL NICKNAME! I WONDER HOW THEY GOT IT? WOULDN'T IT BE GREAT IF, LIKE, YOU HAD A KNOB ON YOUR SINK WHERE FREE SODA CAME OUT? LIKE, THERE'S ONE FOR HOT WATER, COLD WATER, AND ONE FOR SODA!
THAT WOULD BE SO COOL! IT'S "SODA CITY" BECAUSE EVERYONE DRINKS SODA INSTEAD OF WATER! MY MOM WOULDN'T LIKE THAT, BUT I WOULD LOVE IT! THAT WOULD BE COOL! DON'T YOU THINK SO?
I GUESS SO. ONLY, THAT'S NOT WHY IT'S CALLED SODA CITY. IT'S CALLED THAT BECAUSE THE ABBREVIATION OF COLUMBIA IS "COLA" AND COLA IS A KIND OF SODA, I GUESS. SO THAT'S WHY. SEE, NOTHING SPECIAL.

ANYWAY, IT WAS REALLY LATE AT NIGHT, WAY PAST MY BEDTIME. AND IT WAS SO DARK OUT, BUT I WASN'T AFRAID BECAUSE I WAS WITH MY DAD AND POP POP. THAT'S WHAT I CALLED MY GRANDPA. WE WERE OUT IN THE FIELD FOR A LONG TIME AND MY DAD WAS READY TO GO BACK INSIDE, BUT POP POP SAID, "WAIT FOR IT," AND THEN, ALL OF A SUDDEN, LIKE, A THOUSAND . . . OR MAYBE EVEN A MILLION OF THE FIREFLIES CAME OUT OF NOWHERE AND STARTED BLINKING ALL AT ONCE! MY DAD WAS SO EXCITED THAT HE PICKED ME UP AND PUT ME ON HIS SHOULDERS! MY DAD WAS REALLY STRONG! HE WAS THE BEST! AND THEN POP POP STARTED TELLING ME AND MY DAD ALL ABOUT THE SYNCHRONOUS FIREFLIES. HE SAID THERE'S SOME FEELING THAT THEY GET WHEN THEY'RE ALL TOGETHER, LIKE MAYBE THEY FEEL SAFE OR HAPPY WHEN THEY SEE EACH OTHER AND THAT FEELING IS SO STRONG THAT THEY CAN'T HELP BUT LIGHT UP ALL AT ONCE! AND THEN, BECAUSE THEY'RE SO HAPPY, THEY FLASH THEIR LIGHT ALL TOGETHER SO THAT THE WORLD CAN SEE THEIR JOY! AND THAT HAPPENED RIGHT HERE, IN COLUMBIA. SO I GUESS THERE IS SOMETHING I LIKE ABOUT THIS PLACE. IT WAS MY BEST SUMMER EVER.

WELL, I THINK THAT'S ALL WE HAVE TIME FOR. I WANT TO THANK MY SPECIAL GUEST AND COHOST FOR SHARING HIS STORY! TAKE CARE, EVERYONE, AND SEE YOU AGAIN REAL SOON!

EPISODE ELEVEN:
FINDING OUT THE TRUTH

Hey, everyone, welcome to another episode. If you were with me yesterday, I think you saw what I saw: Boogie is definitely not happy. After the brain cast, I went and talked to him, but I didn't want to put that on the show because I wanted him to feel comfortable sharing. He told me a lot of things, and we talked until late at night. To be exact, we talked until three a.m.! I know that was what time it was because we were so loud that Boogie's mom came in and said, "For goodness' sake! It's three a.m., you boys get to sleep!"

*   *   *

Like I said, we talked about a lot of things, some very personal, and they're between me and Boogie. But there are other things that I can share. As a matter of fact, he wanted me to share. He said he thought if you all heard some of his issues that maybe you could help. I hope so.

At first, Boogie actually told me a few fun stories. There was this one with his uncle Cutter. Uncle Cutter owns a few horses . . . How cool is that? And believe it or not, he actually taught Boogie how to ride one. Boogie? The same person who is afraid of a squirrel learned how to ride a horse! He said he's pretty good at it now. I can't wait to see him sitting in a saddle up on a big horse! I promise to show you a brain photo of that.

He did say that he was scared at first to try it, but he said eventually his uncle Cutter helped him find the courage to do it! After that story, he got quiet again, but I kept asking him questions and telling him about things that are going on in my life. And after a while, he brought up the name of this kid he had mentioned to me once before on the phone. The kid's name is Carl, and I could tell just by the way Boogie said his name that he didn't like him. Which, if you know Boogie, is hard to believe. I mean, Boogie likes everyone! And everyone likes Boogie, seriously, everyone! So I started asking him about Carl. I mean, I had question after question about him. At first, Boogie was just kind of quiet or saying basic things like "Yeah," "Uh-huh," or "I dunno," but then out of nowhere he just yelled out, "Carl is bullying me!"

After that, he just started telling me everything about Carl "Out Loud" Dawkins. He said Carl got the name "Out Loud" because he was the type of kid who would say out loud the type of things that most kids would only say in their heads. As he was telling me about Carl, I kind of almost couldn't believe it. My big friend Boogie, the same person who has stood up for me against bullies a whole bunch of times, was being bullied!

*   *   *

At first, I felt bad for him. I mean really bad! I know how it feels to be bullied—it feels terrible! My bully—and I'm not going to say his name because he doesn't deserve any shine on my show—but my bully said so many terrible things about me that I started to feel bad about myself because I believed everything he said was true. But then, one day, my father noticed that I wasn't being myself and had a talk with me.

He said, "Tyrell, when bullies say bad things about you, just know what they're saying has nothing to do with you. It has to do with the way they feel about themselves. Most bullies are sad or afraid and probably feel misunderstood and alone. I know you probably feel anger in your heart for that bully, and I completely understand that. But I tell you what I feel for that bully—I feel sympathy and compassion and truly sad that whatever they're feeling inside is keeping them from being their best self and also preventing them from making friends with a wonderful person like you."

Yup, my dad always knows what to say, and I definitely heard his words, and while I still don't like how my bully treated me, I'm glad my dad helped me to realize that all that stuff my bully said wasn't about me at all.

* * *

But here's the thing: Guess who helped me confront that bully? Boogie! Boogie was standing next to me when I confronted Keith . . . Oops, I didn't mean to say his name. I won't say his last name, but Keith, if you're out there, you know who you are. While I'm no longer mad at Keith, I'm definitely mad at Carl! The more Boogie told me about the things Carl said and did to him, the madder I got! If I'm being honest, and please don't tell my parents this, but I wanted to go and beat Carl up. Of course, that was until I stopped to think about things. I mean, as I've told you before, Boogie is really big, so I started to think to myself if Carl can bully Boogie, he must be reeeally big!

So just before I asked Boogie for Carl's address, I asked him if he had a picture of Carl . . . you know, just so I could know what he looked like. I mean, I didn't want to beat up the wrong person. Boogie pulled out his phone and showed him to me. Guess what? He was pretty small. Now, I'm not trying to small-shame. I mean, I consider myself kind of small, and Carl is smaller than me. I'm just saying I wasn't very impressed.

But before I said to Boogie, "Why don't you just pick him up and throw him," a bunch of thoughts popped into my head. I heard my mom's voice saying, "Violence is never the way to settle things." And I also heard her say, "Someone told me you were thinking of going over there and beating that boy up! Boy, you know better than that!" To which I say, "Which one of you told on me?" I mean, I JUST said that! People, this is a safe place. Please stop telling my mom stuff that I ask you not to share. JUST KIDDING! She didn't say any of that, and as for the rest of that stuff, I was just acting.

But wouldn't it have been pretty wild if that did happen?! Okay, where was I? Oh yeah, my thoughts . . . As I was there looking at a picture of my big friend's little bully, I realized that bullying is not about size—it's about power. Two years ago, I let Keith's mean words have power over me. But after talking to my dad and my friend Boogie, I found the strength in me to take back my power. And then I realized what my mission was . . . to help Boogie take his power back from Carl!

EPISODE TWELVE:
THE BASS REEVES DUDE RANCH

Hey, everyone! Guess where we are?! Don't worry, you don't have to guess because I'm guessing that you wouldn't be able to guess even if I gave you a lot of guesses. We're at something called a "dude ranch," and if I'm being honest, I was today years old when I found out what it is. A dude ranch is a place where you can go and act like you lived in the old Wild West.

You get to eat beans, learn how to use a lasso, sit by a fire, and—wait until you hear this—learn how to ride a horse! Yup, that's right, me, city-boy Tyrell is going to ride a horse! And guess what the name of the ranch is? Oops, I'm sorry that I keep asking you to guess things that you can't really guess. I think I'm just doing that because I'm so excited. My bad!

The name of the place where we're at is the Bass Reeves Dude Ranch! So I'm guessing my horse is going to be really wild! I hope we get to choose the wild level of our horse, I mean, this is my first time and all, and it will probably take me a few times before I become an expert. I think I would choose medium wild to start and then work my way up to wild wild.

* * *

Anyway, Boogie's mom dropped us off a little while ago, and I went into this cabin and they gave me a cool pair of cowboy boots and an amazing cowboy hat! I'll let you see how I look in a minute. I'm just waiting for Boogie to get his Wild West gear. This is really exciting! I feel like me and Boogie could really use a fun day like today. This is going to be awesome! Hey, look at Boogie!

EPISODE THIRTEEN:
THE BIG MESS HOUSE

So, I know we were just doing an episode, but I don't know, this day feels too big to just be one show, so I decided to end the last one and start this one. Now, I'm going to do this episode a little differently. I'm going to narrate it. It's kind of like when me and my dad watch a basketball game and the announcers describe everything as it's happening. If you've ever watched something like that, you know how exciting it can be. I mean, things are just happening, and you never know what's going to happen next. Anyway, like I said, I'm going to narrate, and Boogie will join me on the brain cast as my cohost. Okay, here goes!

EPISODE FOURTEEN:
MOMMY'S LIL RANCH HAND

Welcome back. Well, if you just watched the last episode, you know that things did not go well for Boogie. Actually if I'm being honest, what just happened was one of the worst things I've ever seen, and I once saw my teacher Mrs. Carr sneeze so hard while she was writing on the board that her wig flew off and boogers went everywhere. I mean, that was bad, but this was worse. AND it didn't end there! Since Boogie's clothes were all messed up from the beans, they gave him a shirt from the gift shop to wear. The thing is, the only shirt his size had *Mommy's Lil Ranch Hand* written across the front. And the rest of the day didn't go much better either. When we all went to feed the chickens, for some reason, Boogie's chicken seemed angry and just started chasing Boogie and trying to attack him. Oh, and feeding the goats kind of went the same way! I think the worst thing about the goats for Boogie was that one of them stood up on its back legs and kind of like . . . yelled at Boogie and then ran right at him! And then came the part of the day that we were really looking forward to . . . it was time to ride the horses.

Well, that was all just a lot of "what-ifs" that I really wish had happened. What really happened was when it came time for him to ride, Boogie was the one who froze. And I mean, the sad thing is, like I told you all before, Boogie's uncle Cutter taught him how to ride, so Boogie knows how to do it. And this was his big chance to show off in front of everyone, especially Carl! But like I said, when it was Boogie's turn to get up on his horse, with everyone's eyes on him, especially Carl's, Boogie just stood there and froze! And then Carl "Out Loud" said out loud, "Mommy's Lil Ranch Hand," and everyone laughed.

If I'm being honest, I don't know why everyone keeps laughing at his jokes. They're not funny. They're just mean. Also while I'm being honest, I do not know why the Bass Reeves Dude Ranch sells a shirt that says *Mommy's Lil Ranch Hand*?! Trust me, I know a lot of kids, and none of them would wear a shirt that says something like that.

EPISODE FIFTEEN:
GETTING TO THE BOTTOM OF THE "CARL" THING

Good morning, everyone! Yesterday was terrible! I mean, I came here hoping to cheer Boogie up, and I don't think I'm helping at all. I really tried to cheer him up last night though. I told him all about Al's weird boyfriend, and that made him laugh a little bit. And then I told Boogie he said that me and Shelly should be boyfriend and girlfriend, and then, at the very exact same time, we both said, "Illllll," and that made us laugh so hard that Boogie's mom came into the room and told us to go to sleep.

Oh, and then just as we were falling asleep, I smelled something really bad, and right away I knew what it was, so I whisper-yelled,

"Boogie!! You and those beans!!" And we laughed, but really, that was it. The rest of the night you could tell Boogie was really sad. I was like, "You really should tell your mom about Carl," but he was like, "No, definitely not!" And then he made me promise not to tell her, which I did. I mean, what else could I do?

*   *   *

But this morning, I called my mom and told her. I promised not to tell his mom, not mine. You know me by now: When I have something that's really bothering me, I will usually talk to one of my parents about it. When I have a lot of time to talk, I call my dad because, if I'm being honest, he's kind of slow with his advice. I mean, it's good advice and all, but he likes to sneak in long stories and a bunch of dad jokes. Sorry, Dad, just keeping it real. Now, my mom doesn't play. She gets right to the point, and since I didn't want to get caught on the phone sharing Boogie's business, I called my mom.

*   *   *

I know I haven't been gone a long time, but I was really happy to hear my mom's voice, oh, and Monty's voice. He was barking, so my mom held the phone up so that I could talk to him. It's not easy being away from my family. I actually miss Al yelling at me to get out of the bathroom, but don't tell her. Anyway, I told my mom

90

everything that's going on with Boogie, and she thanked me for sharing it with her. I said that I felt bad sharing Boogie's secrets, and she said that the number one responsibility that I have as Boogie's friend is to make sure that he's okay and that any secret that could wind up hurting him is not a secret that I should keep.

She said anytime I know something harmful, I should look for an adult that I can trust, like a parent or a teacher—you know, people like that—and then let them know what's going on. She also reminded me that she loves Boogie, only she didn't say Boogie—she calls him "Derek"—and that she would have to tell his mom but that she was sure that Boogie's mom would know what to do. Then she told me that she loved me and was proud of me for being such a good and supportive friend.

I told you my mom doesn't play. She got right to the point. My dad would've probably said a lot of the same things, but he would've started out by telling me a story from when he was twelve and his friends were going to jump their bicycles over something dangerous, I don't know, like a firepit or some lions or something like that, and how he didn't think they should and whatnot . . . and it would've probably been a great story, but like I said before, I don't really have time for that. Sorry, Dad.

* * *

When I woke up, I didn't see Boogie, so I went looking for him. When I went downstairs, I saw his mom, and she said he was outside sitting by the stream, so that's where I'm on my way to now. I need to tell him that I told my mom. I know I did the right thing, but I just hope he doesn't get mad at me. This is definitely not going to be easy, so please meet me by the stream for my next episode.

Hey, I guess this is my first actual "streaming" episode. Wow, that was pretty corny. Sorry for that—I'm just nervous. See you soon.

EPISODE SIXTEEN:

STREAMING

SORRY TO CUT YOU OFF, SON! I THINK WHAT TY WAS GONNA SAY WAS THERE'S NOTHING TO BE ASHAMED OF. BOY, I'M YOUR UNCLE CUTTER. I USED TO CHANGE YOUR DIRTY DIAPERS! I LOVE YOU, AND THERE AIN'T NOTHING YOU CAN'T TELL ME.

THERE'S THIS KID NAMED CARL, AND HE'S BEEN KIND OF BULLYING ME. AND YESTERDAY, HE WAS THERE AT THE RANCH, AND WHEN IT WAS MY TURN TO GET UP ON THE HORSE, I SAW HIM STANDING THERE LOOKING LIKE HE WAS READY TO LAUGH AT ME...

... AND THEN I STARTED FEELING LIKE EVERYONE WAS WAITING FOR ME TO MESS UP SO THAT THEY COULD LAUGH AT ME. I COULDN'T DO IT, UNCLE CUTTER. I COULDN'T GET UP ON THAT HORSE. I'M REALLY SO—

I'M GONNA CUT YOU OFF RIGHT THERE, DK. YOU DON'T HAVE ANYTHING TO FEEL SORRY FOR. DO YOU HEAR ME?

YES, SIR.

LOOK, NOW, I HAVE A LOT MORE CHORES TO DO, SO I'M GONNA GET OUT OF HERE AND LET YOU BOYS FISH. BUT I'M GONNA LEAVE YOU WITH THIS: WHEN YOU FALL OFF A HORSE, THE BEST THING TO DO IS HOP BACK IN THE SADDLE.

BUT I DIDN'T FALL OFF THE HORSE.

I KNOW THAT, DK. SEE YOU LATER, BOYS! OH, AND DON'T EAT THE BAIT!

EPISODE SEVENTEEN:
THE MONTAGE

Hey, everyone! Wow, that last episode was a lot! I mean, I don't know if you stayed for the whole thing, but it got pretty deep. Boogie finally spoke to his mom about Carl, which was good. And I got to meet Mr. . . . I mean Uncle Cutter. I know you know he picked me up from the airport in his truck, but he really didn't speak to me. I kind of thought he might be mean and grumpy, but that's not what he's like at all. He's actually very nice and fun! Like my mom always says, "Never judge a book by its cover. Take the time to read it." And Uncle Cutter is definitely a good book.

Oh, and Ricky caught a fish from a stream that wasn't sup-posed to have fish in it . . . and he caught it using a gummy. Yup, definitely a strange episode! But I left this part out! Boogie's mom is throwing me a goodbye party this Saturday and asked us to invite all the kids from Boogie's school, including Carl! Yup, it's already time for me to leave! I'm going to miss this place. I really like it. I wish Boogie liked it too. And I really, really hope this party helps Boogie feel better!

*   *   *

Boogie's mom made some great invitations, and Uncle Cutter took us around to every kid's house to hand them out. It took a long time because things out here in the country are not like things in Brooklyn. In Brooklyn, everyone lives like a block or two away, but down here, everyone lives really far. But Uncle Cutter made it a lot of fun! Wanna see what we did?

Hey, have you seen a part in a movie where the characters have to do a lot of things and they go and do them but we don't see everything they do—we only see the best parts . . . oh, and, like, the whole time everything is happening we hear music? That's called a "montage." Well, that's what I'm going to show you, a montage! I can't really play any music for you, but you can definitely play some music in your head for yourself while you watch my montage. Here goes:

There, I hope you had as much fun watching that montage as we had making it. But if I'm being honest, handing out the invitations wasn't all fun. By the end of the day, we had one invitation left—it was Carl's. When we finally got to his house, it looked sad. I know that's weird to say, but it did.

Before we got out of the truck, Uncle Cutter told us that he knew Carl's family and thought there were some things we should know. He told us that Carl's mom had passed away a year ago, and since then, Carl's dad just wasn't the same. He said Carl's dad used to be bright and cheerful and always had a funny story to tell. But since he lost his wife, he had become a quiet and sullen person.

* * *

So then we got out of the truck and knocked on the door and Carl's dad answered. He kind of looked sad in the same way that I thought his house did. Uncle Cutter said hi and asked to speak to Carl, and then Carl's dad yelled for him. When Carl came to the door, he seemed a lot different than he did at the dude ranch. He seemed way less confident. After Carl got there, his dad asked us what we wanted, and Boogie reached out and handed Carl the invitation. I could tell Boogie was nervous when he did it, because his hand was shaking. Carl looked at the invite and just took it from Boogie without saying a word.

Carl's dad apologized for him and said, "Sorry about my boy's manners. He just never talks anymore since . . . you know. Getting a word out of him these days is like pulling teeth! Anyway, I'll answer for him. I've got work around here for him to do that day, but if he finishes up quick enough, maybe he can swing by for at least the end of the party. All of that is up to him." After that, Uncle Cutter thanked Carl's dad, and then we all said good-bye and left.

* * *

On our ride, Uncle Cutter talked to us about what just happened. He said, "What people show you on the outside isn't always what they're feeling on the inside." Which I thought was really interesting. I mean, when I first met Uncle Cutter, I thought he was mean, and boy, was I wrong. Then Boogie said he thought he kind of understood how Carl felt. He said when his dad passed away every time he thought about him he would feel angry at his dad for leaving. He said he didn't know if he would ever feel happy again!

But then, because he had his mom and people like me in his life, he was able to find a way to feel better. Now when he remembers his dad, he thinks of all the great memories he has, and those memories make him smile. And then he said something that really shocked me! He said he really, really hoped that Carl would come to his party. I know, right? I'll say it again: Boogie is the best. Okay, I'm tired now. I had better go and wash up. Hey, I actually have one more invitation—it's for you! You don't want to miss it. I have a feeling it's going to be epic. See you Saturday!

EPISODE EIGHTEEN:
THE PARTY, PART 1

I'm glad you made it! You're a little late, but that's okay—so am I. This special party episode of the podcast was supposed to start earlier, but I got distracted. Guess what happened? I'm sorry I did that again. I keep asking you to guess things that are impossible to guess. Okay, here it is, you remember how I had to fly here by myself because my parents couldn't get off work to fly with me? Remember? Well, guess . . . I mean . . . um . . . I won't be flying home alone! As a matter of fact, I won't be flying at all! My whole family drove down to pick me up!

*   *   *

I was in the house blowing up balloons for the party, and Boogie's mom called me outside and was like, "Tyrell, there's a minivan pulling up to the house. Does it look familiar?" And it was my dad's van! What?! And as soon as my dad's minivan pulled up in front of the house, the doors opened and out popped my mom, my dad, my sister, and, of course, Monty! I ran over and gave them big hugs, even Al!

Then I picked up Monty and squeezed him, and he slobbered all over me! Then, when Boogie came out of his house to say hi, Monty jumped out of my arms and ran at Boogie and tackled him . . . It really was great!

* * *

So then I was going to start the brain cast, but, like, right then everyone started showing up! I think pretty much every single kid that Boogie gave an invitation to showed up! At first, Monty was the center of attention. Everyone came over to him wanting to pet him or play with him, and Monty enjoyed every second of it. But you know what else happened? As kids were coming over to where me, Monty, and Boogie were, they all started talking to Boogie.

They were telling him things like how they had all been scared of him because to them he was this giant from big, bad Brooklyn and they didn't know what to expect from him. Once Boogie heard that, he just laughed . . . his best, most lovable Boogie laugh! And right there all the kids could tell that they had made a big mistake when they judged the cover of Boogie's book. After that, he answered questions about Brooklyn, told some of our funniest stories, and was a big hit! And you know what else? Boogie looked happy!

After that, we all played a lot of games and ate a whole lot of food! Really, we ate just about all the food . . . just about. My mom made some things at home and brought them all the way from Brooklyn to the party. I don't know if all of you know this, but my mom is, um . . . I'm not going to say she's a terrible cook, but I will say she is creative. And while I ate some, I don't think the other kids were too excited about trying a slice of a New York bacon and cheddar cheesecake, with strawberries and whipped cream.

Anyway, I'm glad you're here! And you're just in time to cut the cake. Boogie's mom wanted me to cut it, but I asked her if Boogie could. She asked me if that's what I really wanted, and I said yes, and then she gave me a big kiss. Anyway, I think I'm going to turn my brain cast microphone on and go live with this one. I'm going to find a good spot to stand so that you get to see everything.

EPISODE NINETEEN:

THE PARTY, PART 2

EPISODE TWENTY:
AFTER-PARTY

Hey, everyone! Okay, that had to be the best episode ever! But for real though, if I had gone live with what happened next, that would've been the best of all time. Don't believe me? First of all, you would think that Boogie's mom and the rest of the adults would've been mad at what happened, but they weren't! They were all just laughing and having a good time. Then everyone even helped clean up, which was even better!

*   *   *

Not amazing you say? There's more! So later Carl and his dad came over to me, Boogie, and Boogie's mom. Carl's dad had his arm around Carl, and he was smiling. And then he was like, "I want to thank you, Iris, for the most fun me and Carl have had in a long time."

He told her how hard it's been for them since Carl's mother died, and she gave them her sympathy and shared stories about how hard it was for her and her sons when her husband passed away. It got kind of emotional, but when it was over, Carl's dad hugged Boogie's mom, said goodbye, and then started to walk away. BUT just before they left, Carl turned around, looked at Boogie, and said . . . wait, no, you've got to see this part. Just watch.

Okay, you can't tell me that wasn't pretty great! Still not the best episode you say? Remember the other day at the dude ranch when Boogie froze and didn't get a chance to ride that horse in front of everyone? Well, what if I told you that right then, all of a sudden, everyone stopped what they were doing because we could see someone was riding on a horse toward Boogie's house? I mean, that person and that horse were going so fast! And what if I told you it was Uncle Cutter on his horse Lucy Bell! And Uncle Cutter and Lucy Bell rode into the party kicking up all sorts of dust!

And what if I told you Uncle Cutter jumped off the horse and then yelled out, "DK, it's time to get back in the saddle! You've ridden this horse before. She knows you and trusts you, just like I do"? And what if I told you Uncle Cutter handed Boogie the reins and I yelled out, "You can do it, Boogie!" and then everyone began chanting, "Boogie-Boogie-Boogie!" even Carl?!

Then Boogie looked at his mom and smiled, and Uncle Cutter put his cowboy hat on Boogie's head and helped him up onto Lucy Bell. And what if I told you that Boogie pulled back on the reins, the horse reared up, and for a moment it seemed like Boogie was going to fall, but just then Boogie smiled and said,

"I'm okay." And right then everyone let out the biggest cheer! And what if I told you that's exactly what happened, would you say that's the greatest episode of *The Tyrell Show* ever? Well then, you said it!

EPISODE TWENTY-ONE:
CONNECTED

Did you miss *The Tyrell Show: Season One?*

Turn the page to read the first few chapters!

EPISODE ONE:
A WORD FROM OUR HOST

Good morning, everyone, and welcome to another season of *The Tyrell Show*. Why do I call it that? you ask. Because I'm Tyrell and this is my show . . . I guess. To all my regular listeners, I say, "Hey," and thanks for joining the livestream podcast that takes place in my head. And for all the new kids listening, thanks for joining me! And I do mean *kids* 'cause if you're an adult checking out my show, let me take this time to share something my mother taught me, "STRANGER DANGER!" There, I had to do that. *The Tyrell Show* is a safe place for me to share my thoughts on my life, and well, having some weird old adult I don't know listening in is definitely not cool.

Okay, glad I got that out of the way. Like I said, this is a new season of *The Tyrell Show*. The minute school was over last spring, I took the summer off from doing my podcast. I had a lot of fun! I went swimming in the neighborhood pool, which was great! Me and my friends only got kicked out four times, which is way better than last year, when we got kicked out twelve times. I guess following the rules is a good thing. Still, I never laughed harder than when my best friend, Boogie, belly flopped into the pool next to Monique. She SCREAMED at him! It was hilarious! We got kicked out for that, and if I'm being honest, I hope we get kicked

out for the same thing next summer. Like I said before, Boogie is my best friend, AND he's kind of a giant, so his splash was epic! He should do it every year. It could be like a big party with food and rides and fireworks . . . we could sell tickets. It would be amazing! If he does it again next summer, I promise to do a special episode of my show so that you can at least hear the splash.

EPISODE TWO:
ALL ABOUT ME AND MY PODCAST

Okay, where was I? Oh yeah, so, like, if you've never listened to my podcast before, I guess I should tell you a little bit about it. On my show, I talk about a lot of important stuff like playing and school and pizza and smelly things, but mostly I talk about me and the people in my life. And you can join me as I share my show in my head while I'm daydreaming, which is pretty much the only place where my sister, Al, can't bother me.

Also I have guests on my show sometimes, only they don't know they're on. Sometimes when they're talking to me I let you hear everything they're saying. Other times I might even imagine something they said and let you hear that too! But really, like I said before, pretty much no one knows about my show . . . except for my best friend, Boogie. He thinks he's my cohost, but really, between you and me, he's not; he's just a special guest. I mean, when you think about it, how would I even let him into my head's recording studio? Maybe through my ear, but unless someone invents a shrinking device I'm guessing that would hurt.

Anyway, I share what it's like for me at home with my family and out in my neighborhood with my friends and even sometimes when I'm in school. Oh, and every now and then, I do "special episodes," like last summer when I did an episode from Disney World! My sister, Al, threw up on Space Mountain, funnel cake and fruit punch everywhere—that was amazing! Hopefully that episode will win an award. And this season I'll be sharing my adventures as I start the sixth grade at Marcus Garvey Elementary. Oh, and not to brag, especially 'cause my dad says I shouldn't, but sixth grade is a pretty big deal—it means I'm one of the big kids now. Us sixth graders are the oldest in the school, and the young kids are probably going to be looking up to us. I'm a little nervous about that. I don't know if you know, but being eleven and a half years old is really hard, and sometimes I worry about a lot of things: Do people like me? Am I safe? What will I be when I grow up? Did Tricia hear me fart in science class? Yup, my show tackles the tough issues that kids like me face each day.

Oh, and I almost forgot . . . the big sixth-grade show! What's that? you ask. Only the most important event ever! It's a show that the sixth graders in our school put on every year right at the end of the first semester. Each year the school comes up with a new theme for the show that's supposed to kind of send out a positive message for our futures. I heard this year's theme is going to be "New Beginnings." I don't actually know what that means, but if I'm being honest, it sounds a little boring.

Last year the theme was "The Fast and the Future," and a lot of the kids dressed up like fast cars and tried to talk like Vin Diesel. It was awesome! I think some of the parents were not very happy with it though, so I guess this year they wanted to make sure the show wouldn't be as fun.

No matter what the theme is I'm excited because ever since I was a little kid I have always wanted to have a big role in the sixth-grade show. Why? you ask. I've gotta say you ask a lot of questions, but if you must know, one reason is that it's kind of a way for sixth graders to leave their mark before they go on to their next school.

They hang pictures of some of the kids from the play around the hallways, and they post videos of the performance online. One time, the news even came to the school and did a story about it, and two of the kids got in a video that went viral. Basically what I'm saying is that it's the most important thing ever! And another reason I want to do it—and don't tell anyone this—is because I'm kind of shy. I mean, I really believe that I would love to perform and have everyone yelling my name and calling me "amazing," but then when I actually think about doing it and really picture it, being up there onstage, I get nervous. But this year I'm going to overcome my fear and get a huge part and have a fan club and get a bunch of followers online. You'll see.

Hey, I just thought about it, most of you new listeners don't really know a lot about me. My dad says it's rude to not introduce yourself when you first meet someone, so I guess I should do that now. My name is Tyrell Edwards, and I think I told you already, but just in case, I'm eleven and a half years old. I think that makes me a tween or at least a pre-tween. I'm not shaving yet, but I keep checking my face for hair— probably gonna come any day now.

Dad calls to me.

That voice you just heard is my dad ... really, I didn't imagine it. He calls me High Speed, which is cool, I guess, only most people think it's 'cause I'm fast ... I'm really not! Not at all, I'm actually

mad slow, I mean "very" slow . . . my mom hates when I speak using slang instead of the proper words—sorry, Mom! Where was I? Oh yeah, slow. When new kids meet me and hear my nick-name, they always want to race me, and no matter how many times I tell them they're faster than me, we still wind up racing and they wind up beating me and saying, "You ain't fast!"

I did win one race though. One time this kid said he could beat me even if he ran backward, which I told him was dangerous,

which he didn't believe, which then ended badly when he ran into a pole. If I'm being honest, I have to say he was way ahead of me when he ran into that pole. My dad said, "Hey, a win is a win!" So like I said, I did win a race once.

By the way, when it comes to the whole "always be honest" thing, my dad says, "Honesty is the best policy, except when your mom asks you about her cooking." So to be honest, when it comes to being honest, I'm a little confused. Honestly, I blame my mom and dad for that. Oh yeah, and speaking of my dad, I never told you why he gave me the nickname High Speed.

He said it was because whenever he asked me a question like "What's the capital of New York?" (Albany) or "How far are we away from the sun?" (between ninety-two and ninety-four million miles, depending on the time of the year), I answered so quickly it was like I was a high-speed internet connection. I guess that was my dad's way of saying I'm smart. The fact is I've always kind of been smart, but being smart doesn't always feel good. Sometimes it feels like no matter what I do, my parents and teachers expect me to do better. A lot of my friends think that I think I'm better than them. That makes me sad—I mean, I just want to be treated like I'm a normal eleven-and-a-half-year-old, but I know that's theoretically impossible . . . sorry for the big word; I use them when I get nervous.

Speaking of nervous, I have to go to the bathroom, so I'll need to end this episode. Trust me, you don't want to come into the bathroom with me. But come back, today is a pretty big day for me. It's the first day of school and I'm already a little stressed out, so really, come back . . . seriously. I'll only be a minute unless Al needs to use the bathroom, in which case I might take a little longer. Okay, talk to you soon!

EPISODE THREE:
MEET MY FAMILY

Hey, everyone. You know earlier I told you all about me, but I didn't mention anything about my amazing family, and, like, that's not cool, so here goes.

My mom's name is Charlene Edwards, and she's thirty-seven, but please don't tell her I told you that. I'm serious! She likes to pretend she's a little younger, and on her birthday whenever any of us make a mistake and say her real age, well, she makes this really scary face, like reeeally scary. I'm just saying it's not something you ever want to see. Anyway, when she's not making that face, she's really pretty and she's extremely nice for an old person, I mean *older* person. She's a social worker, which means she helps people. I think that's a great job for her because she always helps me, my sister, and my dad with just about everything. When we're sick, she knows just what to give us to make us feel better. And whenever we mess up, she knows exactly what to yell, I mean to say, to set us straight. And, um, about her cooking . . . everything is so flavorful and delicious, especially her famous oatmeal raisin garlic cookies. There, that's done. It's always good to say nice things about people, plus my dad gives me and my sister fifty cents every time we compliment her food. Really, I don't know why she puts garlic in them. She always kind of adds in one thing that shouldn't be there whenever she's cooking. With her special cookies, she says, "Garlic is good for you." I don't know if it's good for me, but I know it's not good for a cookie. Um, so I'm not saying my mom can't cook at all. She does make good cereal—I mean, she pours the right amount of milk in the bowl in proportion to the cornflakes. Sorry for the big word, I just got a little stressed again. Then there's:

My dad, Edward Edwards. Ha! Isn't that funny? His first name is almost his last name. That used to confuse me way back when I was a little kid. I thought everyone's first name was their last name. In kindergarten, I told my teacher my name was Tyrell Tyrells. She laughed and my best friend, Boogie, said I cried, but I don't remember doing that; plus, Boogie makes things up. I'll tell you more about Boogie later; right now I'm talking about my dad. He is tall, and strong, and has a beard, like LeBron James, which is why I know my beard is on the way. He's also thirty-seven years old, but he doesn't mind me saying that. And he's a bus driver, or "bus captain" as he calls it. I've been on his bus, and I think he looks pretty cool sitting in his bus captain's chair, like he's in charge. I want to be in charge of something one day. My dad is easy to talk to and always has great advice. And even if I don't always understand what he's saying, I just like the sound of his voice. Sometimes he'll be talking to me and the next thing I know I'll wake up in my bed. I'm not saying my dad is boring, I'm saying his voice has the magical power of sleep with maybe just a touch of boring sprinkled in, which is okay 'cause I love sprinkles. Ugh . . . then there's . . . *don-don-don*:

THE WAY ALEX
SEES HERSELF.

THE WAY
I SEE ALEX.

There's my sister. She's fifteen and sooooo annoying. Her friends call her Alex, short for Alexandra, which she likes. I call her Al, short for Alfred, which she hates. She bullies me, and I tell on her, kind of standard older-sister, younger-brother stuff. People say she's pretty, but I don't see it. Boogie says she's "gorgeous," but Boogie also loves my mom's cooking. She's always getting yelled at for being on her phone. My dad told her that if she doesn't stop staring down at her phone all day, eventually her neck will stay curved forever. To me that's strange because she has a really long neck and long eyelashes, so that just makes me think she'll grow up to be a giraffe. I told that to Boogie, and he said he thinks giraffes are adorable. She can be funny sometimes though, especially when she tells Boogie to get away from her. And, if I'm being honest, I really do like her. I can't say "love" though because, from what I've seen on the reality TV shows she watches, love comes with too much drama.

Sorry about that *butt* thing. Like I said, my parents don't know when they're on my show, or even know about my show at all. Wow, I really lost track of time. There are some other people I wanted to tell you about, but I'll have to do that later. Anyway, I had better get going. I don't want to be late on my first day. I'm going to end this episode now, but tune back in in a little bit and catch me on my way to school.